A NOTE TO PARENTS

Reading Aloud with Your Child

Research shows that reading books aloud ... valuable support parents can provide in helping children learn to read.

- Be a ham! The more enthusiasm you display, the more your child will enjoy the book.
- Run your finger underneath the words as you read to signal that the print carries the story.
- Leave time for examining the illustrations more closely; encourage your child to find things in the pictures.
- Invite your youngster to join in whenever there's a repeated phrase in the text.
- Link up events in the book with similar events in your child's life.
- If your child asks a question, stop and answer it. The book can be a means to learning more about your child's thoughts.

Listening to Your Child Read Aloud

The support of your attention and praise is absolutely crucial to your child's continuing efforts to learn to read.

- If your child is learning to read and asks for a word, give it immediately so that the meaning of the story is not interrupted. DO NOT ask your child to sound out the word.
- On the other hand, if your child initiates the act of sounding out, don't intervene.
- If your child is reading along and makes what is called a miscue, listen for the sense of the miscue. If the word "road" is substituted for the word "street," for instance, no meaning is lost. Don't stop the reading for a correction.
- If the miscue makes no sense (for example, "horse" for "house"), ask your child to reread the sentence because you're not sure you understand what's just been read.
- Above all else, enjoy your child's growing command of print and make sure you give lots of praise. *You are your child's first teacher—and the most important one. Praise from you is critical for further risk-taking and learning.*

—Priscilla Lynch
Ph.D., New York University
Educational Consultant

For Leslie Margulies,
who isn't big *or* bad.
—T.S.

For Grant and Mara Rose
—P.P.

Library of Congress Cataloging-in-Publication Data
Slater, Teddy.
Who's afraid of the big, bad bully? / by Teddy Slater; illustrated Pat Porter.
p. cm. — (Hello Reader! Level 3)
Summary: Big mean Bertha threatens everyone, especially Max, until he gets a dog.
ISBN 0-590-47879-6
[1. Bullies—Fiction. 2. Schools—Fiction. 3. Dogs—Fiction.]
I. Porter, Pat Grant, ill. II. Title. III. Series.
PZ7.S6294Wf 1995 94-3323
[E]—dc20 CIP
AC

12 11 10 9 8 7 7 8 9/9 0/0

Printed in the U.S.A. 23

First Scholastic printing, March 1995

Who's Afraid of the BIG, BAD BULLY?

by Teddy Slater
Illustrated by Pat Porter

Hello Reader!—Level 3

SCHOLASTIC INC.
New York Toronto London Auckland Sydney

CHAPTER ONE:
Who's Afraid of Big Bertha?

Bertha was big. Bertha was mean. Everyone was scared of big, mean Bertha.

All the little girls were scared of Bertha. All the little boys were scared of Bertha.

Even some of the *big* boys were scared of Bertha. She was bigger than they were.

When Bertha said, “Jump!” all the kids jumped.

When Bertha said, “Hand over your candy!” all the kids handed over their candy.

Yes, everyone was scared of big, mean Bertha. But no one was more scared than Max.

Max spent a lot of his time trying to avoid Big Bertha. He took the long way to school . . .

and the long way home.

And he never, ever walked down Dandelion Lane. That's where Bertha lived.

But no matter where Max went, it seemed that Bertha was always just one step behind him.

"I'm going to get you," Bertha called out from behind the old oak tree.

"I'm going to get you," she called out from behind Max's own father's car.

And poor Max was sure
that one day she would.

CHAPTER TWO:
Bully Busters

"You must learn to take care of yourself," Max's dad told him.

Then he signed up Max for karate class.

Max had lots of fun in karate class. He learned how to kick. He learned how to chop.

But the next time he saw Big Bertha, Max did exactly what he always did.

He ran the other way!

“You have to stand up for yourself,” said Max’s brother, Fred. “Just tell Bertha to leave you alone.”

But Max did not think that was a very good idea.

"I bet Bertha would leave me alone if I had a dog," Max told his mother. "A big dog!"

But Max's sister, Lila, was afraid of dogs— especially big ones. So the dog they finally got was not quite what Max had in mind.

Max named his new dog Fang, but he knew he wasn't fooling anyone.

CHAPTER THREE:
Uh-oh, Here She Comes!

Max walked Fang every day. Sometimes he walked Fang around the block. Sometimes he walked him to the park. And sometimes he walked him all the way to Main Street and back.

DANDELION LANE
GRANT RD
STOP

But he never, ever walked him down Dandelion Lane. In case you've forgotten . . . that's where Bertha lived.

One afternoon, Max took Fang to the playground. A bunch of kids were playing baseball there. They all gathered around to see Max's new dog.

"What a cute pup!" said Becky M.

"Isn't he sweet?" said Carole Anne, bending down to scratch Fang's ear.

"What kind of dog is he?" Paul asked.

"He's part Airedale," Max said proudly. "He—"

"He looks more like an air*head* to me," someone broke in.

CHAMP

Max's heart skipped a beat as he recognized the big, mean voice. Slowly, he turned around. And there, right behind him . . . was big, mean Bertha!

Uh-oh, thought Max. Now I'm going to get it.

But Bertha was already looking past him. "Give me that ball," she said to Paul.

Paul gave Bertha the ball.

Max wanted to tell Bertha to leave Paul alone. But when he opened his mouth, not a single word came out.

"Give me that airhead dog," Bertha suddenly said to Max. "I want to see if he's smart enough to catch the ball."

Max wanted to give Bertha a high-flying karate kick. But somehow he knew he couldn't do it.

Bertha took a giant step toward Max and grabbed Fang's leash. "I guess you didn't hear me," she said in her biggest, meanest voice. "GIVE ME THAT DOG!"

CHAPTER FOUR:
Back Off, Bertha!

More than anything, Max wanted to take a giant step back. But he couldn't do that, either. He couldn't leave Fang in Big Bertha's clutches.

There was a long moment of silence. Finally, Max took a deep breath. He yanked Fang's leash out of Bertha's hand and said, "NO!"

Then he took a giant step back.

Bertha could hardly believe her ears. The little kid was actually standing up to her.

Bertha stood there for a moment while she tried to figure out what to do next. At last, she turned to Becky M.

"Give me that mitt," she said.

CHAMP

Becky M. started to give Bertha the mitt. But then she looked at Max. He was still standing there, tightly clutching Fang's leash.

Becky M. snatched back her mitt. If Max could stand up to Bertha, so could she.

Bertha turned to Carole Anne. Carole Anne was busy tapping dirt off her shoe with the bat.

"Give me that bat," Bertha said.

Carole Anne just looked at Bertha. She didn't even stop tapping.

Bertha looked around at all the kids. They were all looking back at her. No one said a word. No one moved an inch.

Bertha was the first to look away. She looked down at the ground, and there was Fang. He looked up at her and wagged his tail.

"*Woof*," Fang said just before he licked Bertha's hand.

"Airhead," Bertha muttered under her breath.

And with that, she turned around and stomped off down the street.

From that day on, Max was no longer scared of Big Bertha. Neither were his friends. As it turned out, once everyone stopped being so scared of Big Bertha, she stopped being so scary.

And by the end of the year, she didn't really seem so big, either!